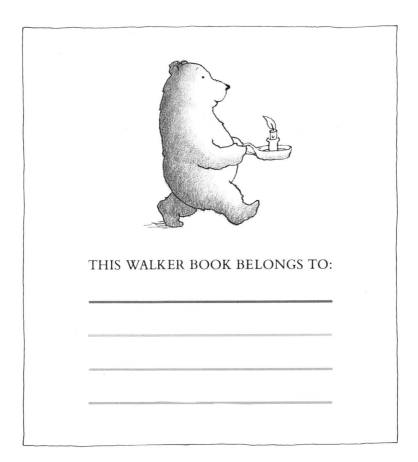

THIS WALKER BOOK BELONGS TO:

For Rhonda

First published 1985 by
Walker Books Ltd
Walker House
87 Vauxhall Walk
London SE11 5HJ

This edition published 1988

© 1985 Jan Ormerod

Printed in Italy by
Lito Roberto Terrazzi, Firenze

British Library Cataloguing in Publication Data
Ormerod, Jan
Sleeping.—(Jan Ormerod's baby books).
I. Title   II. Series
823[J]   PZ7
ISBN 0-7445-0928-9

Sleeping

Jan Ormerod

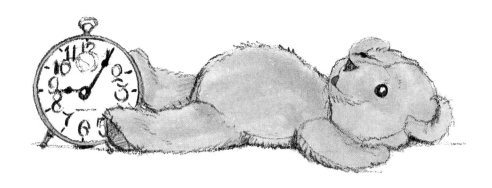

WALKER BOOKS
LONDON

peeping

tickling

climbing up

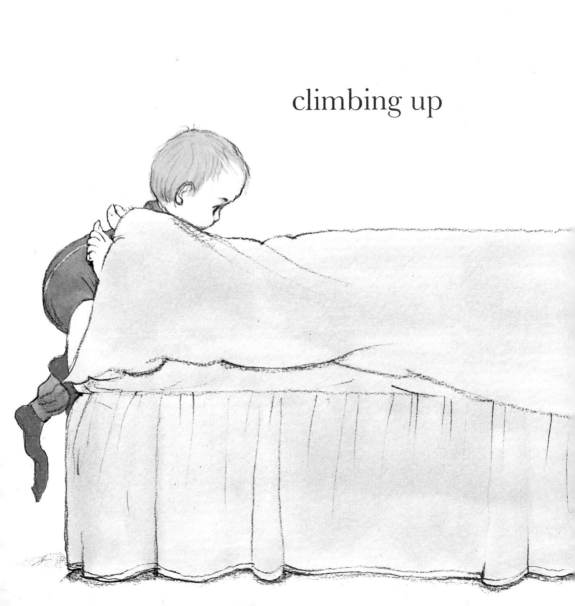

bouncing

pulling his nose

cuddling